ADELE GERAS has been writing children's stories since 1976
and is a highly successful author. Her book, *Troy* (Scholastic),
was shortlisted for the Whitbread award and was highly commended
for the Carnegie Medal. She has had over eighty books published.
This is her first book for Frances Lincoln.
Adèle lives with her family in Manchester.

SHEILA MOXLEY studied art at Bournemouth and Poole College of Art
and graphic design at St Martin's School of Art. *Skip Across the Ocean*,
a collection of nursery rhymes from around the world chosen by Floella Benjamin,
was her first book for Frances Lincoln. It was followed by Saviour Pirotta's
Joy to the World and Heather Maisner's *Diary of a Princess*.
Sheila lives in East London.

Rebecca's Passover copyright © Frances Lincoln Limited 2003
Text copyright © Adèle Geras 2003
Illustrations copyright © Sheila Moxley 2003

First published in Great Britain in 2003 by
Frances Lincoln Limited, 4 Torriano Mews,
Torriano Avenue, London NW5 2RZ

www.franceslincoln.com

First paperback edition 2004

British Library Cataloguing in Publication Data available on request

ISBN 0-7112-2109-X

Set in Cochin

Printed in Singapore

1 3 5 7 9 8 6 4 2

The Publishers would like to thank Bryan Reuben for checking the text and illustrations, and for writing 'About Passover'.

Rebecca's Passover

Adèle Geras

ILLUSTRATED BY Sheila Moxley

FRANCES LINCOLN

Every year in springtime, my brother Josh and I help Granny Sarah prepare for Passover. The festival lasts for eight days, and we eat special foods. The celebrations on the first and second nights are called the Seder.

Josh is six and I'm eight. My name is Rebecca. Granny brings the special Passover dishes out of the cupboard, and I'm allowed to carry them to the kitchen to be washed. My mother told me she used to do the same thing when she was a little girl, and Granny Sarah says when I have a daughter, she'll do it as well. Thinking about this makes me feel happy.

Granny Sarah gave Josh a feather, and told him to look in every
corner and brush away every single crumb of bread. Last year
I asked the Four Questions but this year Josh is more
grown-up so he is going to do it.

While we were helping her, Granny Sarah told us about the Passover.

"Thousands of years ago in the land of Egypt, the Israelites were slaves working for the Pharaoh, the Egyptian ruler. They dragged the heavy stones that built houses and palaces for the Egyptians. They wanted to leave Egypt and live in a place where they could be free."

Granny Sarah told us about God helping Moses. Moses begged Pharaoh again and again to give the slaves their freedom, but Pharaoh refused.

"So God sent the Plagues." said Granny Sarah. "The Plagues were all horrible things, but God sent them to the Egyptians as a punishment for refusing to set the Israelites free. The worst plague was the Slaying of the Firstborn, when the eldest child in every Egyptian family died. We call the festival Passover because the Israelites marked their houses with lamb's blood and the Angel of Death passed over them. This plague was so dreadful that Pharaoh agreed to set the Israelites free."

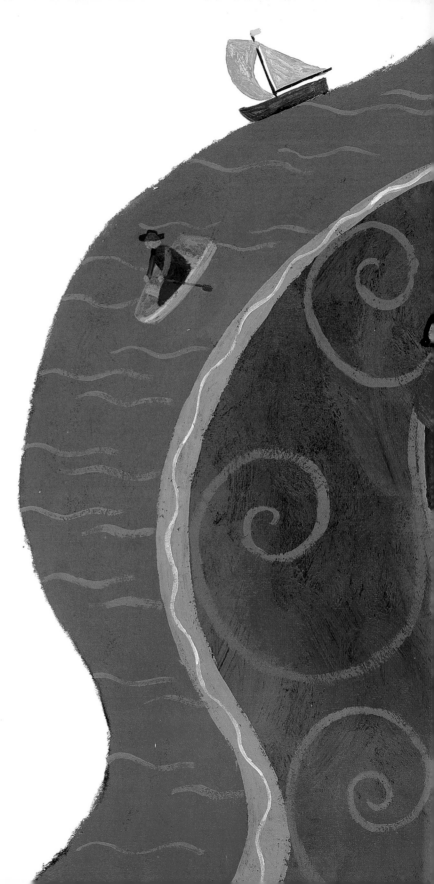

"Moses," Granny Sarah went on, "led the children of Israel through the Red Sea to the Promised Land."

"The sea just rolled back," I said. "Didn't it?"

"That's right," Granny Sarah smiled at me. "Pharaoh changed his mind and set off to chase the Israelites. The Israelites walked along the sea bed with walls of water towering on either side of them. When Pharaoh's army followed them, the sea rolled back and drowned them all."

"But why," I asked, "is the Passover meal called the Seder?"

"Seder means order," Granny Sarah answered, "and the foods remind us of parts of the story, and we eat them in a special order."

"I like the *haroset* best," I said.

"That's good," said Granny Sarah, "because we're going to make some now."

I cut up the apples for the haroset, and Josh mixed
in the chopped nuts. Granny Sarah added some wine
and raisins. The paste was a pinkish-grey colour.
   "It's supposed to look like the mortar they used long ago
to stick the stones of the Egyptian buildings together," she said.
"Now come and help me lay the table."

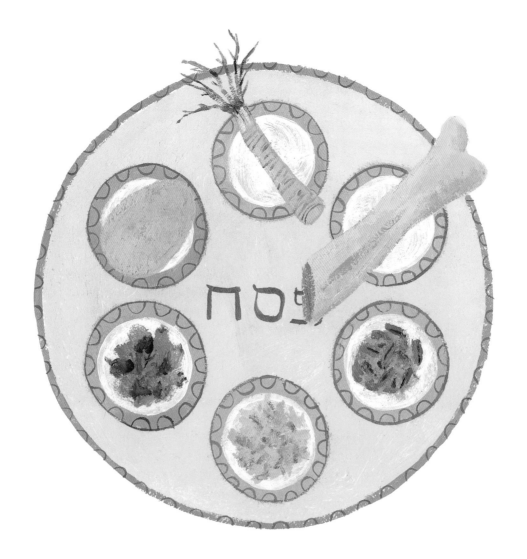

In the dining-room, the table was already spread with a beautiful white cloth, edged with lace. In front of Grandpa Simon's place, there was a big plate called the Seder plate. It had all the special Passover foods on it. Granny Sarah said:

"That horseradish is called *maror*. Its bitter taste reminds us how bitter it was for the Israelites to be slaves. Then there's a bone from a lamb's shank, then the haroset, and then the *hazeret* which are bitter herbs, then *karpas* which is parsley. This makes us think of spring, and the roasted egg reminds us of new life."

"What about *matzah*?" Josh pointed at the big, square crackers on one plate.
"Why don't we eat bread?"

"Because," Granny Sarah answered, "while they were running away, the Israelites
had no time to let their bread rise, so they made matzah which is unleavened bread
and can be made quickly."

"I like them with butter and jam," said Josh.

Granny Sarah and I laughed. "The Israelites didn't have butter and jam, Josh.
Do you remember the *Ma Nishtana*? The Four Questions?"

"Of course I do!" said Josh. "Ben will be old enough to ask them next year."

Apart from our uncle Laurence who lived in Israel, the whole family gathered for the Seder. Our parents, and Granny Sarah and Grandpa Simon and Aunt Ruth and Uncle David with their children, Ben and his baby sister whose name was Debbie. She didn't have a place set for her but there were ten glasses on the table.

"Is that glass for Debbie?" Ben asked, pointing to the extra one.

"She's too young to drink from a glass," said Aunt Ruth, "and besides, she's asleep now. I'm going to put her in her carrycot in the bedroom."

"Who's going to use it, then?" Ben asked.

Grandpa Simon smiled at him.

"We put out an extra wine glass just in case the prophet Elijah comes to drink with us this year."

"Who's Elijah? Have I ever seen him?" Ben asked.

"No," Granny Sarah told him. "He's a prophet who lived long ago. But we hope every year that he'll come and announce the arrival of the Messiah."

Ben seemed happier about the empty glass after that.

During the afternoon, there was a knock at the door. Granny Sarah
went to see who it was, and we all heard her shrieking. She came back
with a big man, who had his arm around her shoulders.

"Is that Elijah?" Ben asked and everyone laughed.

"No, no," Granny Sarah was laughing and crying at the same time.
"It's Laurence, all the way from Israel...
what a wonderful surprise. I must set
another place at the table."
Uncle Laurence smiled.

"Every Passover, we pray the words 'next year in Jerusalem'," he said. "So maybe next year you will come and visit me there. Meanwhile, it's good to spend the festival with my family."

Then the Seder began, and Josh chanted the Four Questions. He looked pale, but his voice sounded clear and strong. The Four Questions ask why this night is different from other nights, why we eat matzah and bitter herbs and why we do things in an unusual way.

Grandpa Simon answered and told everyone that this night was different because we were gathered together to remember that if God had not saved our ancestors from slavery, we would still be slaves ourselves. Everyone followed the story in a book called the Haggadah.

This book told the story of the plagues. These were: rivers of blood, a swarm of frogs, then lice, then wild animals, which was followed by the death of all the cattle, then boils, hailstones, locusts, darkness everywhere, and then the death of every firstborn child. Josh liked frogs and imagined millions and millions of them, jumping out of the river Nile and into all the houses.

As the Plagues were recited, we dipped our fingers in the sweet wine, and made sure to spill a little on the saucer that the wine glass was standing on, to remind us not to be happy at the sufferings of the Egyptians. I sat next to Ben, so that I could help him follow the words.

"What's that, Rebecca?" he asked me, pointing to a picture of a green insect eating a leaf.

"That's a locust," I said. "It's eating the crops."

"Don't like locusts!" he said. "Take them away!"

Aunt Ruth comforted him, and showed him the picture of the frogs. He wasn't frightened of those, even though it must have been very scary for the Egyptians to have lots of squelchy green creatures getting under their feet.

We sang *Dayenu*, a song thanking God for rescuing our people from Egypt.
Then it was time for the feast.

I knew that Granny Sarah had been preparing the Seder feast for days,
and it was delicious. Josh liked the roast chicken best, but I always waited
for the wonderful cake that was different every year. This year, she'd made an
apple and cinnamon cake, and everyone said it was the best they'd ever eaten.

"You say that every year!" Granny Sarah said.

"And every year it's true!" Grandpa Simon answered and everyone laughed.

I was waiting for the best bit of the Seder: looking for the *Afikoman*.
This is half a piece of matzah, wrapped in a cloth napkin. The grown-ups hide it,
and the children have to find it. When we do, we are all given chocolate.
Last year, we found it almost at once, behind the television.

"Maybe it's in Debbie's carrycot," said Josh.

"No," I said. "Aunt Ruth wouldn't want us to wake her up. I expect it's in the lounge somewhere."

Ben was the one who found it in the end, among the leaves of one of the potted plants in the corner. We took it into the dining-room, where everyone was still sitting talking after the Seder meal.

"Time for chocolate, I think," said Grandpa Simon, and went to the sideboard to fetch it. By the time he came back, Ben had fallen asleep with his head on the tablecloth.

"I'll keep his for later," said Uncle David.

"Next year in Jerusalem," said Granny Sarah, looking at Uncle Laurence, and we smiled at one another, thinking of all the families who had come together for the Seder since Moses led the Israelites out of Egypt to the Promised Land.

About Passover

About 3500 years ago, a new dynasty came to power in Egypt and a Pharaoh, probably Rameses II, came to the throne. He enslaved the Israelites and forced them to build his treasure cities Pithom and Rameses. To reduce their numbers, he ordered that all of the boy babies should be thrown into the Nile – but one boy baby was hidden in the bulrushes by his mother, Jochebed. He was found by Pharaoh's daughter, who took pity on him, brought him up in the royal household and named him Moses.

Moses grew up and one day he saw an Egyptian slavedriver ill-treating an Israelite. Moses killed the slavedriver and fled to the desert where God spoke to him out of a burning bush. He told Moses that he was to go to Pharaoh and tell him to set the Israelites free. If Pharaoh refused, God would send plagues to the Egyptians. So Moses returned to Egypt.

Pharaoh was a stubborn man and did not want to lose his workers. With each plague, he agreed to let the slaves go but each time, when the plague stopped, he changed his mind. Before the final, most terrible plague, God told the Israelites to kill, roast and eat a lamb. Then they had to paint its blood on the doorposts of their houses so that the Angel of Death would pass over them. That very night, all the firstborn of Egypt died and Pharaoh agreed to let the Israelites go.

The Israelites rushed out of Egypt so fast that there was no time for their bread to rise, so they baked it unleavened. Today, Jews commemorate the Exodus by eating *matzah* (unleavened bread) and by cleaning their houses to make sure nothing leavened remains.

The Exodus had begun but Pharaoh changed his mind again. He sent his chariots to bring back the Israelites. The Israelites were trapped between the Red Sea and Pharaoh's chariots. Moses stretched his hand out over the sea, and the waters divided. The Israelites crossed safely without getting wet or even muddy, but when the Egyptian charioteers tried to follow them, their wheels got stuck in the wet mud, and the waters flowed back and drowned them.

Moses' sister, Miriam, sang a song of triumph but God reproached her saying, "My creatures are drowning; how can you sing?" The Israelites walked to Mount Sinai, where they received the Ten Commandments, and then followed Moses on the long journey to Israel, their Promised Land.

Every spring, Jews celebrate the transition 'from slavery to freedom' at a special meal (the Seder) and retell the story from a book called the Haggadah. They eat *maror* (usually horseradish), a bone from a lamb's shank, *haroset* (a paste of nuts, apple and wine), *hazeret* (which are bitter herbs), *karpas* (a vegetable – usually parsley) and a roasted egg. At every Seder meal, an extra glass is reserved for the prophet Elijah who, it is believed, will one day arrive to announce the coming of the Messiah.

Recife for haroset

Rebecca, Josh and Granny Sarah make haroset in the story
as part of the Seder feast. Why not make some yourself?

You will need
2 Apples
50g. Chopped almonds or walnuts
50g. Raisins
¼ tsp. Cinnamon
¾ cup Sweet red wine or grape juice

Peel and core the apples and chop finely. Add the raisins and the nuts
to the chopped apples and mix together well. Pour in enough
of the wine or grape juice to make a paste. Add cinnamon to taste.

MORE PICTURE BOOKS IN PAPERBACK
FROM FRANCES LINCOLN

DIARY OF A PRINCESS
Heather Maisner
Illustrated by Sheila Moxley

The Khan of Persia's favourite wife has died and Kublai Khan,
Emperor of all China, decrees that Princess Kokachin shall replace her.
Her escort through the dangerous journey is to be
the famous Venetian, Marco Polo.
This is retold from Marco Polo's 13th Century journals.

ISBN 0-7112-1855-2

SKIP ACROSS THE OCEAN
Floella Benjamin
Illustrated by Sheila Moxley

All over the world, parents entertain and comfort children
with rhymes and lullabies. This is a lively collection
of nursery rhymes from twenty-three countries,
some familiar, some never before written down.

ISBN 0-7112-1285-6

JOY TO THE WORLD!
Saviour Pirotta
Illustrated by Sheila Moxley

Here is a sparkling selection of legends from all over the globe,
each commemorating the Christmas story and gathered from early Christian folklore.

ISBN 0-7112-1572-3

Frances Lincoln titles are available from all good bookshops.
You can also buy books and find out more about your favourite titles,
authors and illustrators on our website: www.franceslincoln.com.